P9-DBM-971

LITTLE FINGERLING

To my granddaughter Melissa, with love
and in memory of E.C.
M.H.

For Nanny, my wonderful
traveling grandmother
B.C.

First published in the United States in 1992 by
Ideals Publishing Corporation
Nashville, Tennessee 37210

First published in Canada by
Kids Can Press Ltd
Toronto, Canada

Printed and bound in Hong Kong

Text copyright © 1989 by Monica Hughes
Illustrations copyright © 1989 by Brenda Clark

Special thanks to Hugh Wylie and Jack Howard of the Far
Eastern Library at The Royal Ontario Museum for their kind
assistance and interest in this book.

Library of Congress Cataloging-in-Publication Data
Hughes, Monica.
    Little Fingerling: a Japanese folktale/retold by Monica
Hughes; illustrated by Brenda Clark.
       p.   cm.
    Summary: A teenaged boy only a finger-length high proves
himself a warrior by vanquishing two monsters with his
cunning and bravery.
    ISBN 0-8249-8553-2
    [1. Folklore—Japan.] I. Clark, Brenda, ill. II. Title.
PZ8.1.H87372Li   1992
398.21'0952—dc20
                                                    92-85
                                                    CIP
                                                    AC

LITTLE FINGERLING

a *Japanese folktale retold by*
MONICA HUGHES
illustrated by
BRENDA CLARK

Ideals Children's Books • Nashville, Tennessee

Once upon a time, in old Japan, there lived a childless couple. Every year, they prayed at the local shrine that they might have a child.

"Even a little child, no bigger than the tip of my finger," the wife begged.

At last their prayer was answered and a son was born to them. He was indeed very tiny, but they were happy and called him Issun Boshi, Little Fingerling.

By the time he was a year old, he was as long as his mother's thumb. By the time he was ten, he was as tall as his father's forefinger.

He grew up happy and resourceful, helping his mother in the house by preparing vegetables and his father on the farm by picking weeds and gathering stray grains of rice.

But when he was fifteen years old and the height of his father's longest finger, he said to himself, "I am a grown man and I have seen nothing of the world but my mother's charcoal stove and my father's plough."

He bowed to his parents. "Honored Father, honored Mother, you have given me a home for fifteen years. You have fed me, clothed me, and taught me all you know. Now it is time for me to go into the world and make my own way."

His mother and father looked sadly at each other and thought, *How can our Little Fingerling make his way in the world? He will be trampled to death beneath the feet of the crowd.* They begged him not to leave the safety of their home, but Issun Boshi was determined to seek his fortune.

But when he was fifteen years old and the height of his father's longest finger, he said to himself, "I am a grown man and I have seen nothing of the world but my mother's charcoal stove and my father's plough."

He bowed to his parents. "Honored Father, honored Mother, you have given me a home for fifteen years. You have fed me, clothed me, and taught me all you know. Now it is time for me to go into the world and make my own way."

His mother and father looked sadly at each other and thought, *How can our Little Fingerling make his way in the world? He will be trampled to death beneath the feet of the crowd.* They begged him not to leave the safety of their home, but Issun Boshi was determined to seek his fortune.

His mother made him a fine traveling costume from a scrap of brocade; and, out of a hollow straw, his father fashioned a scabbard for his sword, which was one of his mother's sewing needles. They also gave him their best lacquer rice bowl and a pair of fine chopsticks.

Issun Boshi bowed respectfully to his parents and set off down the road with his sword stuck in his sash, his chopsticks under one arm, and his rice bowl over his head to keep his fine clothes dry, because it was raining.

Going around the puddles, which were too deep to wade through, he trudged down the path that led from the farm to the road that would take him to Kyoto. His small legs got very tired, and by the time the straw thatch of his parents' house was out of sight, he began to wonder if he had made a wise choice.

But he kept walking. "I will go to Kyoto and make my way in the world," he told himself.

Some time later, he came to a stream crossing the road. *Water flows faster than my legs can trot*, thought Issun Boshi. Quickly he put the rice bowl upon the water, stepped in, and began to paddle with one of his chopsticks.

The little stream joined a river. The river became wide and deep. Still Issun Boshi paddled on, until at last he saw the golden tiles and thatched roofs of the city of Kyoto.

"That wasn't too bad," he said as he jumped ashore and pulled his rice bowl after him. "Now where shall I go to look for work?" he asked himself.

Following the crowds along the streets, he soon found himself in a marketplace. The stalls were piled with rice and fruit, with silks and lacquerware, and with pots and chests and kimonos.

The crowds were so thick that Issun Boshi was in danger of being squashed under a foot or a barrel. In the end, he climbed up the cloth covering a stall that sold hairpins, combs, and useful boxes, turned his rice bowl over, and sat on it to catch his breath.

"Oh, see the little man!" someone cried. In a minute there was a crowd around the stall.

The owner said craftily, "Good people, if you wish to see this fine and unusual sight, the least you can do is to buy some of my poor merchandise."

Everyone laughed and agreed that it was only fair. Before long, the stall owner's table was empty and his pouch was filled with coins.

"What luck brought you to me today?" he asked. "What is your name, if I may ask? And where are you from?"

Issun Boshi explained who he was and that he had come to Kyoto to make his way in the world.

"Then you need look no further," said the stall owner. "Come, join my humble household. You will have a comfortable bed and a full rice bowl. All I ask in return is that you sit on my table during working hours."

"Thank you, honored sir," Issun Boshi said as he stood up and bowed. "But it would not suit me at all to sit idly by. I know that the suit my mother made for me is very fine, as are my sword and scabbard, but they are not worthy of so much comment."

"Then help me with my work, if you wish," the man answered. "Your small fingers will decorate my combs most gracefully. Alas, the man who paints them is old and nearly blind."

So Issun Boshi agreed to work with the stall owner, filling in fine lines with gold lacquer on combs and boxes. In a few months, the stall owner's reputation had spread far and wide.

"What luck brought you to me today?" he asked. "What is your name, if I may ask? And where are you from?"

Issun Boshi explained who he was and that he had come to Kyoto to make his way in the world.

"Then you need look no further," said the stall owner. "Come, join my humble household. You will have a comfortable bed and a full rice bowl. All I ask in return is that you sit on my table during working hours."

"Thank you, honored sir," Issun Boshi said as he stood up and bowed. "But it would not suit me at all to sit idly by. I know that the suit my mother made for me is very fine, as are my sword and scabbard, but they are not worthy of so much comment."

"Then help me with my work, if you wish," the man answered. "Your small fingers will decorate my combs most gracefully. Alas, the man who paints them is old and nearly blind."

So Issun Boshi agreed to work with the stall owner, filling in fine lines with gold lacquer on combs and boxes. In a few months, the stall owner's reputation had spread far and wide.

One day the wife of a nobleman came by, seeking combs for her only daughter's hair. She was fascinated by the sight of Issun Boshi sitting on top of the table, painting the finest imaginable designs in gold on a lacquered comb with a tiny, mouse hair brush.

"Honored sir," she said, "would you consider joining my household?"

"Will you permit me to leave?" Little Fingerling asked the stall owner. "You have kept your bargain. My bed is soft and my rice bowl is always full. Yet I crave a change."

The stall owner sighed. "I shall miss your skillful fingers, but leave if you must. You will go farther with a noble family than with a humble seller of combs and boxes."

Issun Boshi bowed deeply to the stall owner and his wife and hopped into the basket carried by the servant of the noblewoman.

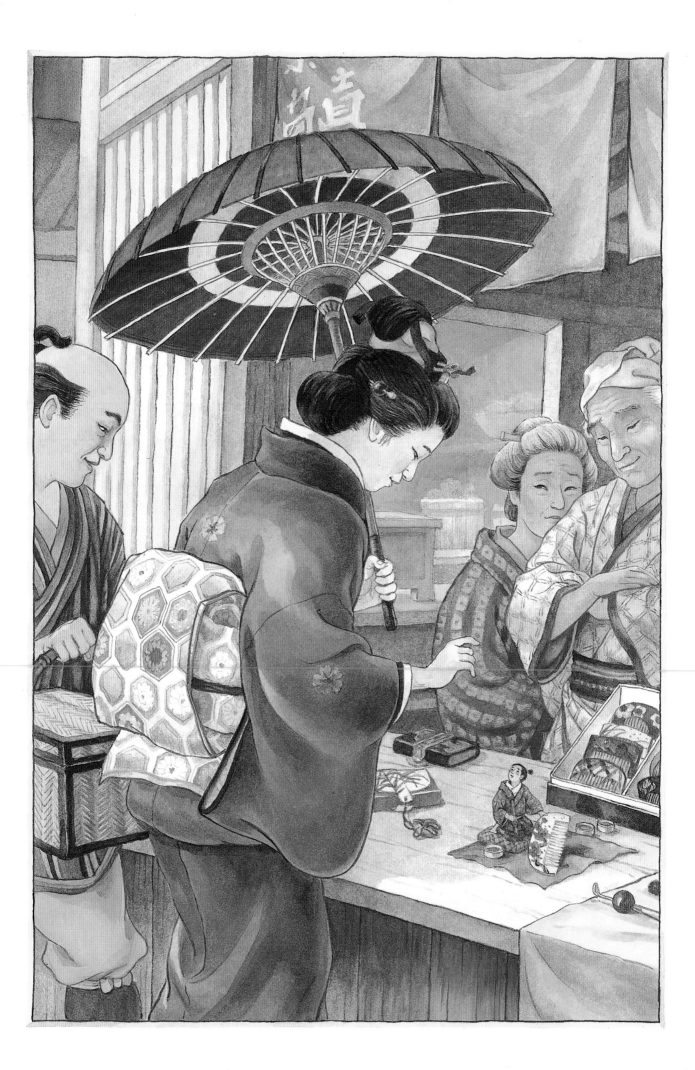

In the house of the nobleman he learned how to read and write, how to fight with a sword, and how to dance; all of the things that the children of the house learned.

They quickly grew very fond of him, and especially charmed was the nobleman's daughter, whose name was Plum Blossom.

One day Plum Blossom wished to visit the temple of Kanzeon, their goddess of mercy. She wished to ask Kanzeon for help, for in spite of herself, she had fallen in love with Issun Boshi.

But how can I give my heart to a person who is smaller than my hand? she silently asked herself. *Yet he is so brave and handsome that my knees shake whenever I see him.*

"You cannot go to the shrine now, Plum Blossom," her mother said. "I am busy and the servants are all making rice cakes for the festival."

"I will go with you, honored daughter of my mistress," exclaimed Issun Boshi, bowing very deeply. "I will protect you with my life." Issun Boshi was secretly in love with Plum Blossom.

The family and servants all hid their smiles politely behind their hands at the idea of Issun Boshi escorting Plum Blossom, but she could not bear to hurt his feelings. "Thank you, Issun Boshi," she answered. "I know I will be safe with you."

They set off along the cobbled streets that led from their house to the temple of Kanzeon. Suddenly a shadow fell across them, and with a horrible cry, two giants barred their way. They were blue all over with horns on their heads, and each had three eyes. One of them swung a huge mallet.

They reached out hungrily toward the beautiful Plum Blossom, who fell to the ground in a swoon. At once Issun Boshi pulled his needle sword from its straw scabbard and leaped nimbly about, slashing at their greedy hands. But there were two of them and only one Issun Boshi, who was far smaller than their littlest fingers. At length one of them managed to grab him between finger and thumb.

They set off along the cobbled streets that led from their house to the temple of Kanzeon. Suddenly a shadow fell across them, and with a horrible cry, two giants barred their way. They were blue all over with horns on their heads, and each had three eyes. One of them swung a huge mallet.

They reached out hungrily toward the beautiful Plum Blossom, who fell to the ground in a swoon. At once Issun Boshi pulled his needle sword from its straw scabbard and leaped nimbly about, slashing at their greedy hands. But there were two of them and only one Issun Boshi, who was far smaller than their littlest fingers. At length one of them managed to grab him between finger and thumb.

Little Fingerling wriggled mightily, but the giant's grasp around his waist was too tight. He was lifted high into the air and popped into the monster's mouth.

It was very dark inside the giant's stomach and his huge heart thumped terribly. Only a little light appeared whenever he opened his mouth to roar.

I must save Plum Blossom, Issun Boshi thought, stabbing his sword into the giant's gullet and pulling himself up. He stabbed and pulled until at last he stood on the giant's tongue. Roaring with pain, the giant spat him out.

Issun Boshi tumbled to the ground, deafened by the roar and dazed by his fall. While he was still stunned, the second giant picked him up and held him close to his face to look at him.

Quickly Issun Boshi stabbed the giant in one of his three great eyes, and with a terrible shriek, both monsters vanished. Again poor Little Fingerling fell to the ground.

"What a terrible fall!" cried Plum Blossom. "Oh, honored friend, are you still alive?"

Issun Boshi got to his feet and brushed himself off. "I am unharmed. But, honored daughter of my mistress, how are you?"

"Thanks to your bravery, I am unhurt, dear Issun Boshi," she answered.

They both blushed and turned away from each other.

"See what the giants dropped in their hurry to be gone!" Plum Blossom exclaimed. "I believe it is a lucky mallet, such as the one Daikoku, our god of wealth and good fortune, carries. They say that when struck upon the ground, it will grant your wish."

"Alas, it is too heavy for me," Little Fingerling said sadly.

"Allow me to strike it for you. What is your wish?"

Issun Boshi looked down and could say nothing, for he knew that it was impossible that he could ever marry Plum Blossom.

"Then I must wish for both of us!" Plum Blossom
cried as she struggled to lift the huge mallet off the
ground and let it fall again.

As she did so the ground shook. The wind blew and the sky grew dark. They both cried out and covered their eyes in fear.

When they dared to look again, Little Fingerling had vanished. In his place stood a handsome samurai warrior. The hollow rice straw was now a magnificently carved scabbard, and the needle his mother had given him had become a samurai sword.

Together the couple walked on to the temple of Kanzeon to thank her for their good fortune. When they returned home, Issun Boshi humbly asked her father for Plum Blossom's hand in marriage.

The nobleman embraced him. "You have always shown yourself to be brave, noble, and resourceful. Now at last you appear as you were inwardly."

So Issun Boshi and Plum Blossom lived happily in Kyoto for the rest of their lives; and Issun Boshi, now no longer Little Fingerling, brought his parents from their farm so that he might care for them honorably in their old age.